In memory of my aunt, Meryl Salter,
and with lots of love to her special unicorns,
Orlaith and Lena—A. R.

For my special unicorn friends
Brielle, Ruby, Bella, Cruz, Isabelle, and Chloe—E. K.

BEACH LANE BOOKS
An imprint of Simon & Schuster Children's Publishing Division
1230 Avenue of the Americas, New York, New York 10020
Text © 2021 by Andrew Root
Illustrations © 2021 by Erin Kraan
Book design by Lauren Rille © 2021 by Simon & Schuster, Inc.
All rights reserved, including the right of reproduction in whole or in part in any form.
BEACH LANE BOOKS and colophon are trademarks of Simon & Schuster, Inc.
For information about special discounts for bulk purchases, please contact Simon & Schuster Special Sales
at 1-866-506-1949 or business@simonandschuster.com.
The Simon & Schuster Speakers Bureau can bring authors to your live event. For more information
or to book an event, contact the Simon & Schuster Speakers Bureau at 1-866-248-3049
or visit our website at www.simonspeakers.com.
The text for this book was set in Belizio.
The illustrations for this book were carved and printed with wood, then colored digitally.
Manufactured in China
0221 SCP
First Edition
10 9 8 7 6 5 4 3 2 1
CIP data for this book is available from the Library of Congress.
ISBN 9781534460058
ISBN 9781534460065 (eBook)

written by
Andrew Root

illustrated by
Erin Kraan

NERDYCORN

Beach Lane Books
New York   London   Toronto   Sydney   New Delhi

FERN wasn't like the other unicorns. Instead of spectacular leaps over shimmering rainbows,

she preferred building robots
in her laboratory.

Rather than splashing majestically
in mountain waterfalls,

she enjoyed coding software
to program her computer.

She liked:

chemistry more
than glitter,

reading rather
than rainbows,

THE MOON

ATOMS AND
MOLECULES

THE SCIENCE BEHIND
ICE CREAM

WELDING

GRAVITY

and 3D printers instead
of sparkles.

CUPCAKE

And even though she knew she was different from
the other unicorns, Fern was proud of who she was.

Because she was:

Smart.
(*Just look at her solve that quadratic equation!*)

A good friend.

(*There she is picking up her neighbor from the airport!*)

And always willing to help others.
(Wow! She's changing their oil and cleaning their gutters!)

But even when Fern went out of her way to do nice things,
some of the other unicorns would still tease her for being different.

They called her names,

occasionally laughed at her glasses,

and never invited her to hang out
with them at the Sparkle Dance Parties.

"I've had enough," Fern said one day.
"I'm through helping rude unicorns."

"The next time they need an engine rebuilt, turbo-sprocket installed, or hydrothermal capacitor welded, they are on their own."

So when Buttercup's sapphire-bejeweled
digital Flutter Phone broke,

Fern kept her soldering iron packed away
and simply shrugged.

And when the wheel on Ruby's
Shimmer Bike snapped,

Fern stood by her truing stand and
centering gauge and just shook her head.

A few days later was the biggest Sparkle Dance of the year.
But Fern decided to stay home.
She doubted the other unicorns
would even notice she was gone.
And besides, she had more
important things to do.

Fern was in the middle of realigning her centrifuge
for a zero-gravity ice-cream experiment
when suddenly she heard a knock.

She opened the door to find Buttercup, Ruby, and the rest of the young unicorns all looking very concerned.

Fern looked at the unicorns,
thought for a moment . . .

and then closed the
door in their faces.

9 scoops
moon rock
salt

3 cups
sugar

6 cups
milk

She went back to her desk and was nearly through
calculating the milk-to-sugar ratio needed to make
ice cream on the moon, when she started thinking
about the Sparkle Dance.

Fern knew the others didn't deserve her help after
the way they had treated her, but deep in her heart
she felt that being

smart,

a
good
friend,

and always
willing to help
others

was far more important than
holding on to a grudge.

Fern gathered her supplies
and rushed to the Sparkle Dance.

Using her
multimeter,

digital calipers,

an arc welder,

two 9-volt batteries,

an old soda can,

some dental floss,

and a bit of dry ice,

she was able to get everything working again.

With the rainbows flowing, the confetti flying, and the starlight shining, every single unicorn cheered for her. She had saved the dance!

they also couldn't wait to put on their tool belts, pull out some graph paper, fire up the acetylene torch, and get to work on one of Fern's amazing projects.

And they each tried their best to be smart,
a good friend, and always willing to help others.